P9-CQG-682

CHILDREN'S THRIFT CLASSICS

The Magic Hat
and Other Danish Fairy Tales

EDITED BY

CLARA STROEBE

Illustrated by Marty Noble

DOVER PUBLICATIONS, INC.
Mineola, New York

DOVER CHILDREN'S THRIFT CLASSICS
EDITOR OF THIS VOLUME: SUSAN L. RATTINER

Copyright

Copyright © 1999 by Dover Publications, Inc.
All rights reserved under Pan American and International Copyright Conventions.

Published in Canada by General Publishing Company, Ltd., 30 Lesmill Road, Don Mills, Toronto, Ontario.

Bibliographical Note

This Dover edition, first published in 1999, is a new selection of nine stories reprinted from *The Danish Fairy Book,* translated by Frederick H. Martens and originally published by Frederick A. Stokes Company, New York, in 1922. The illustrations have been specially prepared for this edition.

Library of Congress Cataloging-in-Publication Data

The magic hat and other Danish fairy tales / edited by Clara Stroebe ; illustrated by Marty Noble.
    p.   cm. — (Dover children's thrift classics)
    Summary: An illustrated collection of nine traditional tales from Denmark including "The little wild duck," "Jack with the golden hair," and "The little girl and the serpent."
    ISBN 0-486-40792-6 (pbk.)
    1. Fairy tales—Denmark. [1. Fairy tales. 2. Folklore—Denmark.] I. Stroebe, Clara. II. Noble, Marty, 1948– ill. III. Danish fairy book. IV. Series.
PZ8.M278   1999
398.2'09489—dc21   99–25113
                                      CIP

Manufactured in the United States of America
Dover Publications, Inc., 31 East 2nd Street, Mineola, N.Y. 11501

Contents

*She passed through the door and found some little people
tending to an ill child.*

The Little Wild Duck

THERE WAS ONCE a woman who had three children; two of them were step-children and the other was her own child. Then the son went away to seek service, and came to the king's court, where he became a prime favorite. The daughters, however, remained at home with the mother. She treated her step-daughter as unkindly as ever she could, and her main ambition was to take her life. Yet the girl was always good and well-behaved, a dear little thing.

One day the step-mother took her and placed her on the edge of the well, and told her to wind yarn, and as she sat there, working away, the step-mother came from behind and pushed her, so that she fell head over heels into the well. But there was not enough water in the bottom to drown her, and she kept looking around the sides of the well until she found an old, rusty door. She passed through it and on the other side found some little people, who were very busy, for it was baking day, and they had a hard time of it because they had a little child, ill and not at all strong, and could not attend to it properly because they had so much to do. So they asked the girl whether she would not mind the child for them a bit; since it was a shame that it should have to cry so. Surely, if they wished her to, said the girl. Well, if she would, said they, it would suit them very well.

So she took care of the child the whole day long, played

with it, and lulled it to sleep, and the child was glad to be with her. In the evening the people said that now she could wish three wishes, because she had been so good to the little one. But she only wished to get out of the well, that was all the wish she had. So the women said since she would not wish for herself, they would wish for her, and she should be helped out of the well besides. So the first wish was, that whenever she took off her hood, and let down her hair, it would grow bright round about her, no matter how dark it might be. The next wish was, that whenever she opened her mouth and blew, a ring of gold would be blown out; and the third was, that if ever she were in danger of drowning, she should not sink, but float on the water in the shape of a little wild duck. When they had spoken her wishes, the people saw to it that she got out of the well, and so she came back to her step-mother.

"What! You're back again?" called out the latter. The girl blew in the air, and a number of beautiful golden rings fell to the floor, and lay there shining brightly. When the step-mother saw this she came running, and tried to pick them up; but the girl quickly picked them up herself, and put them in her pocket. In the evening, when it grew dark, she threw back her hood and let down her hair, and the room grew bright as day. Then her step-mother became more curious, and questioned the girl as to what she had done for the people down in the well, in return for such handsome gifts.

"I'll tell you what I did," said she. "They were baking down below there, and they had a little child, and I took care of it for them, and in return they wished three good wishes for me."

"Then my own daughter must go down to-morrow, and have three wishes granted her, too," said the woman. So the next morning she sent her daughter to the well; and while she was sitting on its edge and spinning, her mother ran up and pushed her in.

At the bottom of the well the girl looked around until she found the rusty door, and came in to the people who lived behind it. This day they were slaughtering and had their hands full. When she heard the child crying, she offered to mind it for them for a while, like her sister. But it was very restless, and she was unkind and angry with it, so that the child grew peevish and cried the whole time; and the more it cried, the more impatient the girl became, and slapped and cuffed it. In the evening she was also allowed to make three wishes, and when she only asked to be let out of the well, since she had had all she wanted of the life below, they said: "You shall surely get out again." And then they earnestly wished for her that whenever she took off her hood and let down her hair, all would grow dark about her, though it were bright daylight; and furthermore, that a fox-tail should grow out of her head, and the oftener it were cut off, the longer it should grow. And then the woman said: "And the third wish is, that whenever you purse your mouth and blow, a gray toad fall to the ground." The wishes had now been wished, and the people agreed that she must be helped out of the well, and so she came back to her mother.

"But what sort of a tail is that hanging from your head?" asked her mother. "We'll have to cut it off." She took her scissors and cut off the tail—it grew longer. Then she cut it again, but this time it grew so long it dragged along the ground after her, and seeing there was no help for it, she had to keep it. After that people called her "Foxtail."

The other little girl's brother served the king, and stood high in his favor. Every day, after dinner, he begged permission to go to the woods. This aroused the king's curiosity, and one day he followed him, in order to find out why he went to the woods every day. And he found that the young fellow had carved a beautiful picture on a tree, a picture of his sister. So the king asked him what sort of a likeness it was, and whether it were an idol to which he prayed? No, said he, it was his little sister at home, and she had a hard time of it because her step-mother treated her so unkindly. Therefore he went out into the woods every day, and prayed the good God might help her, and that life might be made easier for her. At the same time he told the king how beautiful she was, and at last the king said, that if she were so beautiful, her brother had better travel home and fetch her to court, for he might marry her.

So the brother started out, and on the road he bought handsome clothes for his sister, for well he knew that she had but inferior things to wear. And he had luck with his buying, for the new things fitted her to perfection, and she looked beautiful in them. And he delivered the message that she was to come to court in the king's service. Yes, indeed, said the step-mother, and she and Foxtail would go along with them. He could not very well forbid them to go, so all four of them started on their journey.

When they were out at sea—for they had to take ship to reach the royal castle—it stormed so that the brother came on deck, and said to his sister: "Take good care of yourself!" For the waves fell inboard, and swept the deck in a terrifying manner. But she could not hear what her brother said, for her step-mother had boxed her ears so severely that she was hard of hearing. So she asked her step-mother: "What did my brother say?"

"He said you were to take off your dress, and give it to my daughter to put on." Whatever her brother told her to do the girl did gladly. So she took off her dress, and exchanged it for that which Foxtail had been wearing. Not long after her brother once more cried: "Sister, take good care of yourself!"

"What did my brother say then?" she asked.

"He says that you are to take the jewels from your head, and give them to my daughter." Well, she was glad to do whatever her brother told her, she said, and took the jewels from her own head and put them on that of Foxtail. But they did not show to such advantage there because of the tail on her head. Then her brother called out once more to her: "Little sister, do take good care of yourself!"

"What did my brother say?"

"He said that you were to lay your head in my lap, so

that I might comb your hair," said the mother, and the girl did so, since whatever her brother told her to do she was glad to do. That very moment, however, her step-mother threw her into the sea.

Yet she did not drown, but turned into a little wild duck, and swam after the ship.

When they landed, the king came down from the castle to meet them, and asked whether this was his sister. For now, of course, the brother had only his step-sister with him. And the king grew angry when he saw her, and said the brother should be cast into the serpents' den, and there the serpents should devour him. That was the punishment in those days for a person who had done some great wrong. So they cast him into the serpents' den as the king had ordered.

Now at nightfall there came a little wild duck, and swam up the drain-pipe so that she reached the king's kitchen, and there she flung off all her feathers, and warmed her poor, naked little body by the fire. A little dog was sitting in the kitchen, and the duck went up to him and said:

"Rowzer, Towzer, under the bench!
Is the king in his castle asleep?
Is the old rogue asleep behind the stove?
Is my brother asleep in the serpents' den?
Is my sister Foxtail asleep, and her mother as well?"

Then she threw a rod to the dog, which he was to give her brother to ward off the serpents, and finally she blew out a golden ring for the kitchen-maid, because she had allowed her to warm herself by the fire.

Now as a matter of fact, an old rogue had been lying behind the stove; but he had been awake, not asleep, all the time, and listening. At last, when the duck had drawn on all her feathers again, she said: "I will come twice more, and if I am not delivered then, I will have to pass the rest of my life on the seashore."

The rascally old servant heard that, too; but he did not

venture to tell the king, because if it did not turn out to be true, he was afraid he would also be cast into the serpents' den.

On the following evening the duck again appeared, swimming up the drain-pipe to the kitchen as before. When she came into the kitchen she shook off her feathers, and said to the dog:

> "Rowzer, Towzer, under the bench!
> Is the king in his castle asleep?
> Is the old rogue asleep behind the stove?
> Is my brother asleep in the serpents' den?
> Is my sister Foxtail asleep, and her mother as well?"

And at the same time she threw him a rod to give to her brother, so that he might ward off the serpents; and then she blew out a golden ring for the kitchen-maid to reward her for letting her warm herself. At last she said: "Now I shall come once more, and if I am not released then, I will have to pass the rest of my life on the seashore."

The old rogue was lying behind the stove as before, and heard everything, and the next day he told the king all that had happened, and all that he had heard. So the king decided to lie behind the stove himself and listen, and if what he heard did not agree with what his servant had said, the latter would have to go into the serpents' den.

And at nightfall the little wild duck came swimming in through the head of the drain-pipe, as usual, and said to the dog:

> "Rowzer, Towzer, under the bench!
> Is the king in his castle asleep?
> Is the old rogue asleep behind the stove?
> Is my brother asleep in the serpents' den?
> Is my sister Foxtail asleep, and her mother as well?"

Then she threw a rod to the dog to give her brother so that he might ward off the serpents, and blew out a golden ring for the kitchen-maid, because she let her warm herself. "Now I will never come back again, and will have to spend the rest of my life on the seashore," she said, and waddled along the floor as ducks do. But she had shaken off her feathers, as usual, when she came; and these the king had taken secretly, while she was going up and down, and now she needed her feathers and could not find them at all. So she began to complain bitterly: that now she did not even have her feathers, and she would be sure to freeze, since she could no longer come and warm herself in the kitchen. Yet the moment came when she had to go, and she was about to swim out through the drain-pipe as usual, when the king seized her, and though she tried to escape, he held her firmly. Then she turned into a cheese, and when the king laid the cheese into the ashes of the hearth, the cheese turned into an eel. Then the king took a knife to cut off its head, when suddenly it was changed into the loveliest maiden he had ever seen. First of all they sent to release her brother from the serpents' den, where the serpents had done him no harm, because he had been innocent when cast into their lair. Then Foxtail and her mother were seized, and had to admit all they had done against the little wild duck, her brother and the king. And they were punished and came to an evil end.

But the king married the lovely maiden who had been the little wild duck, and her brother is in the king's service to this very day.

The Little Girl and the Serpent

THERE WAS ONCE a little girl who had to take her father's dinner out to him in the fields, where he was working. And when she had brought him his dinner he told her to go fetch his jacket, which he had laid under a tree. And the little girl went to fetch it. But when she came to the tree, there was a monstrous big serpent lying on the jacket, so she took a stick and made as though to drive him off; but the serpent would not leave the jacket. Then the girl begged the serpent please to go away, so that she might take the jacket to her father.

"Yes," said the serpent, "if you will come back and seat yourself on my back, you may take away the jacket."

The girl agreed, the serpent crawled off the jacket, and the girl brought it to her father. Then she came straight back again, and seated herself on the serpent's back; but no sooner had she done so than the serpent crawled to the woods, and kept crawling further and further into them.

After they had gone a long way, the serpent said: "Little girl, stand up on my back and tell me if you see anything?"

The girl stood up and said: "I see something shining like bright silver!"

"Yes, that is my mother's castle," said the serpent. "We still have a long way to go."

Then the serpent crawled through the woods for another long stretch, and once more said: "Little girl, stand up on my back and tell me if you see anything?"

"Yes," said the girl, "I see something shining like pure gold!"

"Well, that is my father's castle," said the serpent. "We still have a long way to go."

So the serpent crawled on again for a long stretch, and said for the third time: "Little girl, stand up on my back and tell me if you see anything?"

"Yes," said the girl, "I see something shining like diamonds!"

"Well, we will be there in a moment," said the serpent. And he crawled on until he came to a handsome castle, and there he laid himself before the door, and said to the girl: "Stand on my back and ring the bell! And when the doorkeeper comes, tell him you want to take service in the castle; then he will receive you kindly."

The girl did as the serpent told her, and when the doorkeeper came and asked her what she wanted, she told him that she wished to take service in the castle. He asked her what she could do, and she said she could sweep the floor, and carry water and help in the kitchen. Then she had better come right along, said he, for they could make good use of her. So he led her into the castle, and showed her to her bedroom, and then she went down to the kitchen and helped with all the work, and everybody took a liking to her because she was so active.

In the evening, when she came to her little room, she heard some one knock at the door, and asked who it might be. "Oh, just myself," replied the serpent. "It is so cold out here that I am freezing. May I come in and lie down in your room?" The girl felt sorry for the serpent, who had to lie outside and freeze, and she let him in. But no sooner was he in the room than he tried to kiss her. She held her apron before her face, but the serpent kissed her for all that, and suddenly he was changed into as handsome a prince as one might wish to see. He thanked her for releasing him from his enchantment, and told her that he was a king's son, and that they were in his own castle. The prince and the maiden now celebrated their wedding with great pomp, then went to see his father and his mother, and after that visited the parents of the little girl, whom they brought back to the castle with them, where they all lived in peace and happiness.

Jack with the Golden Hair

ONCE UPON A TIME there was a fisherman who made his living fishing. One day, when he was out casting his nets, a bad storm came up, and it so happened that a merman swam up to him and asked him whether he would like to get home. "Yes," said the fisherman, he'd like to get home very much, but it did not look as though he would, since the weather was so bad, and he was alone in his little boat. "Well," said the merman, "if the fisherman would give him the youngest thing in the house when he got home, he should have good weather and fisherman's luck; and he would not demand the youngest thing in his house from him for full twelve years. Yes, said the man, the merman was welcome to the youngest thing in his home, for he thought that such a condition might be susceptible to change.

The weather at once cleared up, and the fisherman caught so many fish that their number was past belief. Then he sailed to a trading port and sold them, and put out to sea again to catch more. He returned to port several times, sold his fish, and collected a great deal of money.

At home his wife had been mourning for him, because he had not returned with the other fishermen, and she thought he was dead. The others put out to sea again when the weather changed, and there they came across him, standing in his boat and hauling in the fishes as fast as he could.

"God be praised, there you are safe and sound!" said they. "Your wife has been mourning for you, because she feels sure you have been drowned."

"She need not worry about me," said the man, "for I'm going home to her now." He had money, he had fish, and he had all sorts of things that he had bought in the city, and so home he went. But when he came home there was a little baby boy waiting for him—the youngest thing in the house. The fisherman said nothing about his talk with the merman, and that he would have to give up his child after twelve years. His fisherman's luck was constant, and he earned a great deal of money. In the course of time he bought a little farm and kept two horses.

The boy who had come into the world during his father's absence at sea, grew up and became strong. His name was Jack, and as soon as he was big enough, he learned to handle the plough. When his father was alone with the boy, he often had to cry. Once, when the boy was nearly twelve years old, he asked his father why it was that he always cried. So his father told him it was useless to conceal it any longer, how he had been caught in a storm at sea, and had been obliged to promise a merman the youngest thing he would find in the house when he got home. But the merman did not want him until he was twelve years of age. The boy's twelfth birthday was near at hand, and he had to tell his wife. She would not be comforted: they had only this child, and now they were to lose it, and to lose it in such a way.

But Jack himself said: "I have no objection; if he wants to have me, he will probably do me no harm." And when he was about to leave, and his mother said that at least he ought to put on his best clothes, Jack answered: "No, if he wants me, let him clothe and feed me, too!"

So his father took him out to sea, to the appointed place, where the merman was to receive him. And the merman came and took the boy with him, and his father went back home again, and his fisherman's luck remained constant as before.

Now when Jack came down to the merman's abode, all he had to do was to take care of a horse and a lion; it was his business to spread fire before, and oats behind them.

Every day the merman drove his goats into the wood, and in the meantime Jack was left to shift for himself, and as has been said, was supposed to take care of the two animals.

One day the horse said to him: "That's not the way to do! You should lay the fire behind and the oats before us!"

"What!" cried Jack, "are you able to talk?"

"Yes," said the horse, "I have known how to talk for a number of years; but if you are true to us, you can deliver us and yourself as well."

"That is just what I'll do!" replied Jack.

Then the horse said: "Go into the great room! There you will see three bottles standing on the table, and a great sword hanging from the wall. Drink first from the one bottle, then from the next, and finally from the third. And then see whether you are able to lift the sword. And there is a comb lying on the table with which you must comb your hair."

Jack did as the horse told him. He went into the room, and there he saw the bottles. On the first one was written: "If you drink from this bottle you will be strong." And when he had drunk from it he was able to move the sword a little from its place. Then he took the second bottle. On it was written: "If you drink from this bottle you will become stronger." And when he had drunk from it he found he was able to lift down the sword from the wall. Then he took the third bottle. On it was written: "If you drink from this bottle your strength will be measureless." And when he had drunk from it, he tried the sword, and found that he could swing it with ease. Then he took the comb and combed his hair; and his hair grew so long that it reached to his heels, and it shone like gold. Then he returned to the horse, and told him he had done as he had been told, and that now he could swing the sword.

Then the horse said: "Now you must pack up all the eatables, and as much gold and silver as we can carry, and then put on the kirtle hanging on the wall, and gird on the

His hair grew so long that it reached to his heels.

sword." Jack did all this, mounted the horse, unloosed the lion, and rode off, the lion running after.

In the evening, when the merman came back with his goats, he found Jack, the horse and the lion gone. He grew furiously angry and began to pursue them. Then the horse said to Jack: "Turn around and look back!"

"It seems to me as though the sky were getting quite black and gray behind us," said Jack.

"Yes, it is the merman, who is chasing us," replied the horse. "Tear a hair out of my tail, and one out of my mane, and order so great a forest to grow behind us, that the merman will not be able to pass through, and will have to go home to get ax and saw, in order to chop his way through."

And the merman came to the forest, and had he not been furious before, he would surely have become so now; for he had to turn back and get ax and saw in order to chop his way through the trees. Now they had a long, good start; but suddenly the horse said: "Turn around and look back!"

"Yes," said Jack, "it again seems to me as though the sky were getting black and gray behind us; but it is much worse this time than before."

"Tear a hair out of my tail, and one out of my mane," said the horse, "and order so deep a sea to spread out behind us, that the merman cannot pass through it until he has brought his goats to drink it up."

When the merman reached the sea, he grew still more furious, ran back home and brought his goats to drink it up. Now they had another long, good start. After a while the horse said: "Look around once more. Is there anything to be seen?"

"Yes," said Jack. "Now it seems to me as though there were a fire burning behind us, high up in the air."

"Well," said the horse, "the merman is really furious now. He is so furious that one could strike sparks from his eyes. Pull a hair out of my tail, and one out of my mane, and order such a hot fire to burn behind us that the merman cannot cross it unless he goes home and fetches his steel pole to help him leap across."

So the merman had to go back and fetch his steel pole, and he nearly missed finding it. He looked in every nook and corner, and at last came to his old mother, who sat in one of them.

"What is the matter, little son?" said she. "Why are you so angry?" For he darted about everywhere dealing blows and punches. Well, said he, it was not to be wondered at that he was angry: the lad whom he had brought up, had stolen all his property, and though he had pursued him, he could not reach him; first he had planted a forest in front of him, and the second time a sea, and now it was a fire; and he could not cross the fire unless he found his steel pole, to help him jump across.

"Heaven above!" cried the old woman. "Had not I better go along with you? I think I could jump more lightly than you could!"

So he took her on his back and dragged her along. When they came to the fire, he thrust the pole into the middle of it so that the old woman could take hold and jump across; and she jumped and jumped right into the flames. There she sat and cried: "Heaven above! little son, do come and help me out of the fire!" So he jumped into the fire in turn, and there they both sat and were burned up.

Then the horse said: "Well, now we are rid of the merman. Can you give us something to eat? For we are hungry, and whatever you can eat we can eat as well." When they had eaten, the horse spoke again: "There is a king's castle here in this forest. You can go there and take service; but you must come out here every evening, and bring us something to eat."

Jack went to the castle and was taken in as a stable boy. He had to wash, groom and curry the horses, and the head groom was very well satisfied with him. When they gave him his supper in the evening, he took it out into the forest to the horse, who asked him: "Well, what luck did you have, Jack?"

"I'm in the stable," said Jack, "and they treat me very well indeed."

"That will never do," said the horse. "You cannot stay there. To-morrow, after you have washed the horses, rub dust and straw into their coats."

And Jack did as he said. The following morning, after he had washed and curried the horses, he took dust and straw and rubbed it into their coats. The head groom came and saw what he had done, grew angry, took his whip and gave Jack a terrible flogging. When the cook of the castle saw that, he felt sorry for the boy and he said: "It is a sin and a shame to beat the little fellow so unmercifully!" No, said the head groom, he had deserved it, because he had rubbed dust and straw into the horses' coats after he had washed them.

"Give the boy to me," said the cook, "I can make good use of such a lad."

So Jack came into the kitchen, where he was even better placed than he had been in the stable. He was given leavings of bread and meat and his supper as well, and could take it all out to the horse. In the evening he went into the forest, and told him what had happened, that now he was in the kitchen, and was treated very well. But the horse said: "That will not do either; you cannot stay there. To-morrow morning, after you have cleaned and rinsed, you must dirty the dishes again, so that they will drive you out."

"But then I'll get such a hard beating," said Jack.

"You must pay no attention to that," said the horse, "you will be compensated for your beating in due time."

And Jack did as the horse told him. The next day, after he had rinsed the dishes, he dirtied them again. When the cook saw this he fell into a rage, seized his poker and gave the boy a good thrashing. Jack cried and wailed till the gardener came along and heard him.

"Why, how can you beat that poor boy so?" he cried.

"Because he is so mischievous," said the cook. "First he rinses the dishes, and then he dirties them again."

"Give me the little fellow," said the gardener. "I can make good use of him in the garden."

So Jack went to the garden with the gardener, and in the evening, when he had been given his supper, he ran out into the forest to the horse.

"I'm in the garden now, and they treat me very well," said Jack.

"Well, see to it that you stay there," said the horse. And Jack was glad to hear him say so, for he had no mind to change service again as he had been doing.

Jack stayed with the gardener and was well treated, and every evening he went out to see the horse. The king had three daughters, and the gardener was accustomed to make up a bouquet for each of them every Saturday. On the first day that Jack was there he begged the gardener to let him make up a bouquet. But the gardener would not risk it; he was afraid that Jack would not attend to it properly, and he had just enough flowers to answer his purpose. But Jack begged and begged until finally he was given permission, and he made up a little bouquet which was much prettier than any ever made up by the gardener. And now they had to bring the bouquets—Jack wanted to deliver his in person—to a certain door, through which the princesses passed at a given hour, and received the flowers. Here Jack saw the princesses for the first time, and he looked carefully to find the one to whom he would best like to give his bouquet, and lo and behold, it was the youngest princess! Jack was wearing an old dirty cap, that covered his wonderful hair, and this cap he never took off. When he came to the door where the princesses and the courtiers were standing, he was told to take off his cap.

"No, I am scabby!" said Jack, and from that time on every one called him "Scabby Jack." And when the royal family would go down into the gardens and walk there, they often amused themselves by saying to Jack: "Take off your cap!" for then he would always answer: "I am scabby."

So he gave his bouquet to the youngest princess, and she tipped him with gold pieces. He showed these to the gardener, and said how odd it was that she should have given him counters. Then the gardener relieved him of the gold pieces, and gave him copper coins instead; for those he recognized.

When Saturday came around again the gardener wanted Jack to make up all three of the bouquets; but Jack would only make up one, and that he gave to the youngest princess. She told him again to take off his cap, but he again said no, that he was scabby. So she tipped him again with gold pieces for which the gardener gave him copper coins. Time passed, and people began to tease the princess about Scabby Jack, and she had to hear his name every hour of the day.

Now it happened that a war broke out, and the whole country was besieged by the army of the foe. All who had not already gone to the war then wished to take part in it, and every one was given a horse. Scabby Jack asked for a horse, too; but there was nothing but an old mare left, who could only move on three legs. So they gave the mare to Jack, and he rode off on the three-legged beast, with every one laughing and grinning behind his back. He rode away from the others into the wood, where the horse and the lion had stayed, and where he had hidden his sword and kirtle. There he hid his ragged old jacket and his old cap, tied his three-legged mare to a tree, and mounted the merman's horse. His golden hair hung down his back, he had his sword at his side, and the lion followed him. In this wise he rode to the battle-field, and halted a short distance away to see how matters stood. The enemy was so powerful that he was about to gain the upper hand. So the horse said to Jack: "Blow into the handle of your sword!" And soldiers rose from the earth in such numbers, horsemen and footmen, that one could not see the ground. Then Jack hewed about him with his sword, and the lion bit and clawed, and they slew many of the enemy. And when the enemy had been defeated the horse said to Jack:

"Now blow into the other end of your sword!" And then all the soldiers disappeared. An armistice was then proclaimed until the following day, when the battle was to continue.

The king ordered his people to bring him the man who had won the battle. But Jack rode back into the forest, and they could not find him. When he got there, he unsaddled his horse, hid his kirtle and his sword, stuffed his wonderful hair under his cap, got on his three-legged mare and rode back to the castle. He was the first to get back, and was able to tell all that had happened; how some one had come with a great number of soldiers and had beaten the foe.

On the following day the same thing happened. Jack came and asked for a horse, so that he might ride out and look on. Well, said the king, since he was to be his son-in-law some day, he would have to give him a horse. For that was the jest that they played on the youngest princess, saying that she was to marry Scabby Jack. So he was once more given the three-legged mare, rode out to the forest, tied her to a tree, and mounted his own horse, with his sword at his side, his golden hair hanging down his back, and the lion following after him. Thus he rode on and drew rein by the king's army, and watched the enemy slay the king's soldiers. Then the horse said to him: "Blow into the handle of your sword!" And soldiers rose from the earth in such numbers, horsemen and footmen, that it was impossible to count them. And Jack hewed and thrust, and the lion bit and clawed so many of the foe that the latter were again defeated. Then the horse said: "Blow into the other end of your sword!" And the soldiers, every last man of them, disappeared.

The king and his people were well aware that the same person had helped them once more, and they rode after him; but he reached the forest before any one caught up with him. The king could not understand where the soldiers who had aided him came from, for he had asked no other nation's help. Jack unsaddled his horse again, hid his kirtle and his sword, stuffed his hair under his cap, put on his old rags and rode home on the three-legged mare. He was the first one to get back, and all crowded around him to hear what had happened. Jack informed them that strange troops had once more appeared, and had aided them and defeated the enemy. There was an armistice declared until the third day, and then the battle was to be resumed.

When the others rode off, Jack also wanted to go along and watch. And, as he had the last time, the king said that Jack should have a horse, since after all, he was to become his son-in-law. The three-legged mare was the only horse left, and was once more given to him. He rode to the forest, took off his old jacket and put on his war mantle, mounted his own horse, and with his sword at his side, his golden hair hanging down his back, and followed by the lion, he drew rein by the army and looked on. Now this day the king himself took part in the battle, for he wanted to end the war. And the enemy were about to capture the king, when the horse said: "Blow into the handle of your sword!" And at once so many soldiers rose from the earth, horsemen and footmen, that they hid the ground. Jack rode upon the enemy, hewed and thrust, and the lion bit and tore to pieces all who got in his way. This went on till not one of the enemy was left, for they had all fallen. Then the horse said: "Blow into the other end of your sword!" And all the soldiers, every last man of them, disappeared. The king had them blow the alarm, to encircle the stranger, whoever he might be, for he was the same who had now appeared for the third time. And they formed so thick a ring around Jack that he saw no way out. Yet it seemed to him he could glimpse a little gap in the ranks near the king, and he tried to break through there; but the king struck out at him so lustily that he wounded him in the leg. Nevertheless, Jack rode quickly to the forest, unsaddled his horse, hid his sword, put on his old clothes, stuffed his hair beneath his cap, mounted his three-legged mare again, and was the first back at the castle.

When he reached home the youngest princess was standing in the door, and asked how her father had fared; for she well knew that matters must have come to a serious pass when he himself had gone to battle. Jack told her that the same stranger who had already twice appeared, had come again that day, and had destroyed the enemy to the last man; but no one knew who he might be. Jack's leg was bleeding, and he asked whether she could not give him something to tie around it. The three-legged mare had run into a tree with him in the forest, he said. The princess had a silk handkerchief in her hand, embroidered with her name, and she gave it to him to tie around his leg. Then the others came back from the war, the king among them, and the war was over.

Now the king had not the slightest idea of where he was to look for the stranger who had aided him, though he much desired to know who he was. So he had them proclaim in his own and in every other kingdom that whoever had been wounded in the leg should have his daughter and half the kingdom, and after his death the whole of it, if he could appear in the costume worn by the unknown stranger. And high and low came from his own kingdom, and from foreign countries. Many had wounded themselves in one leg, others in another; they thought perhaps that would answer, and that they would receive the princess and the kingdom and be made kings. At last they had all appeared, but not one could show the wound given by the king. Now there was only Scabby Jack left, who had also looked on at the battles, and had ridden the three-legged mare. So he was told to put in an appearance, though he said it was foolish, since he had only ridden out on the old three-legged mare, and looked on. But he had to show himself, nevertheless.

When he came to the castle, the servants said to him: "Take off your cap, Jack!"

"I am scabby," said Jack. He went on and came to the king.

"Take off your cap, Jack!" said the courtiers, "the king wants to speak to you."

"I am scabby," said Jack. The princesses were in the room in which he was to show himself, and both the older princesses nudged each other, and laughed at the youngest: here was Scabby Jack, surely he was the one who had defeated the enemy, and now he would get his princess. The king greeted Jack and said, this was his son-in-law coming, he had been to the wars as well as the rest, and wanted to show himself. A couple of courtiers who were standing there helped him show his leg. Yes, said he, he knew he had a bad leg, the old three-legged mare had run against a tree with him in the forest. The king wished to see the wound, and when it came to be exposed, there was the princess's handkerchief wound around it. And if they had not already teased her enough about Scabby Jack they did now, and every one had his joke. But when the king had looked at his leg he saw at once that it was the very wound he himself had made. He gave Jack's cap a knock, so that it rolled all the way to the door, and his golden hair fell down over his back. Then the king said: "You are not the man we thought you were. I see that we were mistaken in you."

Now his leg was properly dressed, so that it would heal again, and the king told him to come to him in the same costume he had worn in battle. For he saw that Jack had been his deliverer, and that he had the right to choose the one he preferred among his daughters. Jack begged him to wait while he went to the forest, and promised to be back in a jiffy. So he hurried there and threw away his old rags, for which he had no further use. Then he went to the horse and told him all that had happened. Yes, said the horse, he knew all about it. Then Jack asked the horse which of the king's daughters he should choose.

"You must take the youngest," said the horse, "they

made fun of her because of you, so she is the one you should choose."

Then Jack put on his cloak and mounted the horse. With his sword at his side, his golden hair hanging down his back, and the lion following after, he rode to the castle. And now it was plain to all that he was the one who had played the hero in the war. Every one went to meet him, and the king asked which one of his daughters he wanted. Jack answered, just as the horse had told him to, that he chose the youngest, because they had made so much fun of her on his account that now he liked her best of all. The wedding-day was set and Jack was made king.

The horse and the lion were led to the stable, and Jack went there every day to talk to the horse, which ate just what Jack did. On his wedding-day Jack was down in the stable with the horse, as usual, when the latter said to him: "Now that I have rescued you from the merman, and helped you to make yourself king, will you deliver me?"

Why, of course, was Jack's answer, he would if he could possibly do so.

"Then you must chop off my head, and put it where my tail is, and you must chop off my tail and put it where my head was."

"I cannot do that," said Jack, "you have been so kind to me that I could not treat you so."

"If you do not do it," said the horse, "you shall once more be just as unhappy as you were when the merman was after us."

So Jack had to do it. But no sooner was it done than the horse turned into the handsomest prince one could wish to see. He went up into the castle with Jack to see the king, and the king recognized him at once—he was the crown-prince of his own land. And the king was much alarmed, for he had already given the kingdom to Jack.

"That makes no difference," said the prince, "for if it had not been for Jack, I should never have been delivered. And if I had not been delivered, then Jack would never have become king; so I do not begrudge Jack the kingdom."

And the prince remained Jack's friend and trusty counsellor. The lion was a lion, and remained a lion, who went to war with them, and overcame all who fought with him. But the fame of the sword had become so widespread that after a time none dared to go to war with Jack, and all of them spent their lives in peace and quiet.

Peter Redhat

THERE WAS ONCE a princess, yonder in England, who was so beautiful that none might compare to her, and she actually had it printed in the papers; but at the same time she was so haughty that she scarcely recognized herself. The king, here in Denmark, had a son, who also had a good opinion of himself, and it occurred to him to set forth and sue for the princess's hand. So he took ship and set sail with a great retinue. When he reached London, he went to the castle and told the king of his intentions. The king said he had no objection, save that the princess must have a free hand in the matter, and so they called her. But when the prince made his proposal, she threw back her head, and said she no more wished to have any dealings with him than with her father's blacking-brush or blacking. And with that he was at liberty to march off.

Now he decided that he would play a trick on her in payment for her answer. So he went back to his ship, and had his things brought ashore and placed in a room which he had hired, and instructed his people to sail home and tell his father he would not be back for the present.

Then he told his servant to go to town, find the shabbiest vagabond to be met with, and change clothes with him. The servant went up and down the streets, and there saw many a poor devil; but it was his task to find the most wretched-looking of all. At last he heard voices in a cellar and went down. There sat a fellow called Peter Redhat, and he was the raggedest the servant had seen thus far. The servant asked whether he would change clothes with him. But Peter Redhat grew furious, because he thought the other wished to make a fool of him. Yet he was quite

25

in earnest, and so the change was made. Peter had an enormously large, broad-brimmed hat, known throughout the city; and this the servant obtained as well. Back he went to the prince with these clothes, and all was satisfactory.

In the meantime the prince had visited a goldsmith, and had ordered a golden distaff, a golden spindle, and a golden yarn-reel, and when they were ready he put on Peter Redhat's clothes and went with his golden distaff to the king's garden. There he sat down and began to spin beneath the princess's windows. When she awoke and saw Peter Redhat sitting there, spinning with a golden distaff, she sent down one of her maids to him, with the princess's compliments, to ask whether she could not buy the distaff from him. Yes, it could be done, but he wished to speak to her himself. She did not much care to do so, yet she had never seen anything quite so handsome as the distaff, and she wanted it so much that she made up her mind to go down to Peter. Then she asked him what he asked for the distaff. All he wanted was permission to sit in her room for a night. The princess was half inclined to be angry, and turned on her heel with the words: "No! Fie, for shame, that such a pig should sit in my room! That cannot be." But that was the only way she could obtain the distaff, said he, for he would not sell it for money. The princess looked at the distaff, and her wish to possess it grew stronger, and the longer she looked the more she wanted it; till she felt that she simply could not go on living without the distaff. So she discussed with her ladies-in-waiting whether the matter might be arranged. They decided that it might, if he were willing to promise to remain seated in one and the same place, and they remained on guard in the room overnight.

So she received the distaff, and at evening Peter Redhat came and sat him down on a chair near a little table. There he sat all night long, and did not move from the spot. In the morning he had to leave, so he went down and took his golden spindle. The princess slept late, and when she awoke she saw Peter Redhat sitting in the garden, reeling the yarn that he had spun the day before. When the princess saw the spindle she sent down one of her maids, with her compliments, to ask whether she could not buy the spindle from him. Yes, the princess could buy it, but he wished to talk to her himself. So she came down to him, for she wanted the spindle very much, and it seemed to her that it must be joined to the distaff.

"What does it cost?" she asked him. It cost no more than the permission to sit overnight by the side of her bed.

"Fie, for shame! Peter Redhat sitting beside my bed," cried she, "that would never do!" But she could get the spindle no other way. So she went in to her ladies-in-waiting, and asked whether they did not think that he might be allowed to sit beside her bed, if all twelve of them sat there too, and three or four lights were placed on the table, because she had such a desire to obtain the spindle. And they decided that if they put the table, with five lights on it, close to the bed, and then stationed themselves around the table, close to the bed, it might answer. So she got the spindle, and Peter Redhat came that evening and sat down in a chair beside the bed in which she lay. But the princess did not sleep much that night, because Peter Redhat sat there and looked at her the whole night through.

When day dawned he had to leave again, and this time he went home and took the golden bobbin, for now he had to wind the yarn that he had reeled the day before. The princess slept somewhat late; but when she awoke and came to the window, there sat Peter Redhat, diligently winding yarn. She at once fell in love with the bobbin, for she had never yet seen one so beautiful, and if she could obtain it she would have the complete spinning-set. She sent down one of her ladies, with her compliments, to ask whether she could not buy the bobbin. Yes, surely she could buy the bobbin, but he himself wished to talk to her. So she had to come down to Peter for the third time.

"What does the bobbin cost?" she asked him. No more than permission to lie at the foot of the princess's bed that night.

Fie, for shame, that Peter Redhat should lie at the foot of her bed! That could never be! And she grew angry. But there was no other way of getting the bobbin, and so she consulted her ladies-in-waiting about it. They thought that if she placed twelve chairs along the sides of the bed, and one of them were to sit on each chair with a lighted candle, it might be done, for, of course, they knew what the princess wanted. The princess received the bobbin and at evening, when she had gone to bed, Peter Redhat came. She lay as close as she could to the wall, and he was ordered to lie as closely as he could against the foot of the bed. Then he began to undress, and he flung one garment here and another there, and his big red hat he threw in front of the door. Then he lay down and at once began to snore, so that the walls shook.

Now the ladies-in-waiting had been on guard for two nights in succession and, one after another, they fell asleep, and the candles fell from their hands, and went out and at last there was only a single light left burning— all the other ladies were sleeping. Then the princess said that since he was sleeping so very soundly, the light might be put out, if only the ladies would be ready to come should she call them. But the ladies were not called, and all of them slept so very late, right into the next forenoon, that the king himself came to wake his daughter. But when he opened the door he could not get in, because of Peter's hat, which he first had to shove aside. The king recognized the hat at once, and became furiously angry. Peter Redhat had to get up, into his clothes and be off as soon as possible; and then came his daughter's turn. She was banished from the country and had to leave that very day. So she had to make the best of it and see that she got away. Some money was given her, but it was far too little, since she now had to look out for herself, and was not used to traveling alone. When she drove off, Peter Redhat sat up behind, and when she stopped at an inn to remain overnight, Peter Redhat stopped there too. She saw to it that she had the best of everything, but Peter Redhat lived as simply as possible.

On the following day she drove on, and so it went for several days; while Peter always saw to it that he kept pace with her. In the course of time the princess's money came to an end, and she had to go a-foot. Peter took a couple of good sandwiches with him and when the princess started out, he started out at the same time. He passed her and said good-day, but she did not answer him, and would not even glance at the side of the road on which he walked. In the evening they reached an inn, and she was given the best room, while Peter had to be satisfied with one less than second-best. On the following day he passed her again, and when he said good-day to her, she was at last able to look around and thank him. Then he asked her whether she would not like to have a sandwich. Yes, she would, for her money was going fast; soon she would be unable to pay for a night's lodging. Then Peter said he would pay for her. They came to an inn and left it again the following morning. Then he told her that he could not keep on paying her way because his money was also coming to an end. They came to a river and had to cross, and Peter paid for both. When they had crossed, it was evening, and again they had to look for a place where they might spend the night. They were in the prince's own country by this time, and they came to a forest close to his father's castle. Now the princess had to thank God that she had Peter Redhat; for there was no one else upon whom she could lean, and they found a tiny hut in the woods, where they stayed.

"What shall we do now? We have not a single shilling left?" She did not know what to suggest. "Then there is nothing left for us to do," said he, "but wander about and beg; for, of course, we cannot steal."

So they agreed to meet at the hut once or twice a day. She made a little bag to hold meal, and grits and breadcrusts, and then they separated and each went his way for the day.

Of course the prince went home to the castle, and brought back a large purse of gold in his pocket; but she wandered about and gathered such scraps as the people gave her, and in the evening they met in the hut. He asked her what she had taken in, and she showed him: a few pieces of bread, a little meal and grits, and a few bits of meat.

"Oh," said he, "you do not bring back much when you go a-begging! Just see what I have!" And he drew the big purse with all the money in it from his pocket, and said that it was what he had collected that day.

"But it would be best for us to take service somewhere."

Yes, she was willing, was her answer.

"Well, what work can you do?" he asked her.

She would prefer to find a place as a seamstress.

He did not know whether she could manage to get a place as a seamstress, but he did know where they would take her in to wash dishes. The fact was that the following day there was to be a great banquet at court, because the prince had returned and, to judge by what the people said, there would be a wedding.

Then he made her believe that he had found employment at the castle as a wood-chopper, and so he would be able to have her out in the kitchen. "But could you not arrange to bring me a pot of soup at dinner-time from what is left on the table?"

"Yes, but how am I to manage to carry it to you without attracting attention?" said she.

"You can tie a cord around your waist, under your apron, and hang the pot on it."

She thought she could manage this, and he told her which way to go in order to meet him.

In the morning she went up to the castle and began her work. They gave her a pair of old kettles to scour, and she nearly scoured them to pieces; but the prince had told the cook in advance that a girl would put in an appearance at

a certain time, and that he was to give her plenty to do,
but she was not to be otherwise molested, and they were
not to push, beat or handle her ungently. When the court
had eaten dinner, the kitchen-maid asked permission to
go to town for a while; and filling a little pot with soup and
meat, she tied it under her apron, and started out to find
Peter Redhat. She had to pass several doors at which
guards were standing, who invited her to come in and
dance with them; for on that day whoever wished to was
allowed to enter the great hall and dance. But she excused
herself, saying that she had no time to spare. At last she
saw the door through which Peter had told her to pass,
and there some one seized her, and dragged her into the
hall where the banquet was in progress. The prince came
up at once, and led her out to dance, and she had to yield,
willy-nilly. But she did not recognize him, for he was wearing his princely clothes. The music began, and the prince
danced with her so lustily that the dumplings and scraps
fairly rolled all around the floor. Every one wanted to
know whose they were, because a number of others were
also dancing. But she at once admitted that she was
guilty. She had a sweetheart, she said, who was employed
in the castle, and she had been on her way to him with a
little pot of soup. Then the king asked her which way she
had been told to take. Her sweetheart had told her she
should pass through the door at the right-hand side of the
castle gate. Then the king asked her again whether she
would recognize the man again if she saw him. Indeed she
would recognize him, for they had traveled many miles
together.

"Then pick him out," said the king, "for here are all the
people who are employed in the castle." No, he was not
among them, said she. But the king kept on talking to her,
and meanwhile the prince stole out of the room, put on
the old clothes he had worn while they had been together,
went outside and walked past the window at which she
stood. Then she pointed him out and said: "That is my
sweetheart walking there." Thereupon he came in to

When the prince danced with her, the scraps rolled all around the floor.

them, and the king himself could hardly recognize him as he now appeared. He said to the princess: "Do you not think it might have been better for you had you taken the king's son out of Denmark, of whom you made so much fun?"

"Ah, do not speak of it," said she, "I have trouble enough as it is."

"Yes, but if he is still willing to take you, do you think he would be good enough for you?"

"It would be wonderful, no doubt, but that opportunity will never recur."

"And yet it might," said he, "if you promise me that you will never again be ruled by arrogance and haughtiness."

Then he told his father and guests that this was the princess for whose sake he had traveled to England; and that he had played a trick upon her because she had been so arrogant when he had sought her out the first time, and had not been willing to so much as look at him. But now he was convinced that she had changed, and that the time had come when she should know who he really was, and be raised from her low estate. So they brought her garments, and he laid aside Peter Redhat's rags, and the wedding was held at once. Since he was the crown-prince of the land, he became king after his father's death and she, as was no more than right, became queen. But her parents always held a grudge against him because he had humiliated her.

The Princess with the Twelve Pair of Golden Shoes

THERE WAS ONCE a young man who had wandered out into the world to seek his fortune. As he went his way he met an old man who asked him for alms. The lad told him that he had no money; but that he would gladly share with him what food he had, and this the old man gratefully accepted. They seated themselves beneath a tree, and the young man divided the food into two equal parts. When they had eaten he rose to go on his way; but the old man said: "You shared what you had with me, and in return I will give you this stick and this ball, for they will make your fortune. If you raise the stick in the air in front of you, you will become invisible; and if you strike the ball with the stick, it will roll in front of you, and show you the road you should take."

The young man thanked him for his gifts, cast the ball to the ground and struck it with the stick. The ball rolled swiftly in advance of him, and kept on rolling, until they came to a large city. Here he saw that the chopped-off heads of human beings had been planted all around the city walls. He asked the first person whom he met why this was, and learned that the whole country grieved because of the princess, who wore out twelve pair of golden shoes every night without any one knowing how she did so. The old king was weary of it, and had vowed whoever could solve the mystery should receive the princess and half the kingdom beside; but whoever tried and could not solve it would have to lose his life. Now many princes and great lords had come and made the attempt, because the princess was surpassingly lovely; but all of them had had to yield their lives, and the old king was in deep sorrow because of it.

When the young man heard of this he had a great mind to undertake the adventure. He at once went to the castle and said he would make the attempt the following night. When the old king saw him, he felt sorry for him, and he advised him to give up the undertaking, since he was certain to have no better luck than his predecessors. But he held to his resolve, and the king said that he should sleep for three nights in the princess's room, and see whether he could discover anything; and if he had not discovered anything by the third day, he would have to take his way to the scaffold.

The young man was satisfied to have it so, and in the evening he was led into the princess's room, where a bed had been prepared for him. He leaned his stick against the bed, hung his knapsack on it, and lay down resolved not to close an eye the whole night. He stayed awake for a long time and did not notice anything; but suddenly he fell asleep, and when he woke up it was bright daylight. Then he was very angry with himself, and resolved firmly that he would keep a better watch the following night.

But the next night passed just as the first had, and now the young man had but a single night left.

When he lay down the third night, he pretended to fall asleep at once; and before long he heard a voice asking the princess whether he were sleeping. The princess answered, "Yes," and thereupon a maiden clad in white came to his bed and said: "I will test him, at any rate, to see whether he is really asleep," and she took a golden needle and thrust it into his heel. But he did not move, and she went away and left the needle behind her. Then he saw her, together with the princess, move aside the latter's bed, so that a flight of stairs came to view, and they went down the flight of stairs. He rose quickly, took the needle and put it in his knapsack on his back, and held his stick before him so that he was invisible. Then he followed them down the stairs, and they went on until they reached a forest that was all of silver—trees, flowers and grass. When they came to the end of the silver forest, he broke a branch from a tree, and put it in his knapsack. The princess heard the trees rustle and turned around; but she could see no one. "Oh, that is only the wind!" said the maiden with her.

Then they came to another forest, where all was of gold—trees, flowers and grass; and when they reached the end of the golden forest, he broke a branch and put it in his knapsack. The princess turned around, and said it seemed as though some one were behind them; but the girl replied again that it was only the wind.

Then they came to a forest whose trees, flowers and grass were all of diamond, and when they reached the end of the diamond forest, he broke a branch from a tree and put it in his knapsack. Finally they reached a lake, and there lay a little boat, and the princess and the girl got in. But as they were about to push off, he leaped into the boat, and it rocked so strongly that the princess grew afraid, and cried out that now surely some one was behind them. But the girl replied it was only the wind.

They crossed to the opposite shore, and there lay a great castle. An ugly troll came up, received the princess, led her in and asked her why she was so late. Then she told him she had suffered a great fright, and that some one had followed them, though she had seen no one. Then they seated themselves at the table, and the young man stood behind the princess's chair. When she had eaten he took away her golden plate, her golden knife and her golden fork, and put them all in his knapsack. The troll and the princess could not imagine what had become of them; but the troll wasted no more thought on them, for now he wanted to dance. So they began to dance, and the princess danced twelve times with the troll, and each time she danced with him she completely wore out a pair of golden shoes. But when she had danced the last dance and thrown the shoes in the corner, the young man picked them up, and put them in his knapsack. When the dancing was over the troll led her back to the boat, and the young man crossed with them, and was the first to jump ashore and run home swiftly, so that he got there before they did, and could lie down in bed and pretend to be asleep when the princess arrived.

In the morning the old king came, and asked whether he had discovered anything; but he said he had fallen asleep, as he had the two nights preceding, and had not noticed anything. This made the old king very sad; but the princess was all the happier, and wished to see him beheaded herself. So the young man was led to the scaffold, and the king and the princess and the whole court went along.

And as he stood on the scaffold, he begged permission of the king to tell him a wonderful dream he had dreamt during the night just passed, and the king granted his request. So he told how he had dreamed that a girl clad in white had come to the princess and asked her whether he was asleep; and in order to make certain, the girl in white had thrust a golden needle into his heel. "And I think this is the very needle," he said and drew it forth from his knapsack. "And then I dreamed that they pushed the princess's bed aside, and went down a flight of steps, hidden beneath the bed, and I went after them; and then I dreamed that we came to a forest where the trees, flowers and grass were all of silver, and I broke a branch from one of the trees. Here it is. Then we came to a forest where the trees, flowers and grass were of gold, and I broke a branch from one of those trees. Here it is. Then I dreamed we came to a forest where the trees, flowers and grass were of diamond, and I broke a branch from one of those trees. Here it is. Then I dreamed that we went on and came to a lake, where lay a boat, and the princess and the girl got into the boat. But when I leaped in the princess was frightened, and said that there was some one behind her, though she could not see me. We crossed the lake to a great castle, and there an ugly troll received the princess and led her into the castle, and sat down to dine with her;

and I dreamed that I stood behind her chair, and that after she had eaten, I took her plate, her knife and her fork and put them in my knapsack. Here they are. And then I dreamed that the troll asked the princess to dance with him, and that she danced twelve times, and each time she danced she wore out a pair of golden shoes. But when she had danced the last dance, and flung the shoes aside, I picked them up, put them in my knapsack, and here they are. Then I dreamed the princess came home again; but I reached the castle before she did, and lay down in bed before she arrived."

When the old king had heard all this his happiness was beyond bounds; but the princess was half-dead with fright, and could not imagine how it had all happened. The king now wished the young man to marry the princess; but he decided to pay the troll a visit first, and asked the princess to lend him her golden thimble. She gave it to him, and the young man descended the stairs, passed through the silver forest, the golden forest and the diamond forest by the lake, and rowed across to the troll's castle. When he found the troll he thrust him through the heart with the golden needle that he had drawn from his heel, and held the princess's thimble beneath it. Three drops of blood fell into it, and the troll died.

Then he rowed back, and when he came to the diamond forest, he let one drop of blood fall to the ground, and at once all the trees, flowers and grasses turned into as many men, women and children, who were so happy to be released from their enchantment they begged him to be their king, for they were a whole nation. They followed him to the golden forest, and there he let another drop of blood fall to the ground; and there, too, all the trees, flowers and grasses turned into human beings, enough to people a kingdom. They went with him to the silver forest, and here he let the third drop of blood fall to the ground and all the trees, flowers and grasses likewise became human beings, praised him as their deliverer, and wished to make him their king. They went with him to the old king and told him of their deliverance, and he and the princess were also happy, now that she, too, had been released from her enchantment. Then the wedding was celebrated with great splendor, and he became king over all three kingdoms.

The Magic Hat

ONE DAY a shepherd boy was sitting on a hill. It was the very day that they were celebrating a big feast in the neighboring village; and when the bells rang at noon—as was always the custom in the old days—he heard a great tumult and noise inside the hill upon which he was sitting, and the same question asked, over and over again: "Where is my hat? Where is my hat?" That seemed strange to him, and suddenly it occurred to him to call out himself: "Have you no hat for me?"

"No," said one voice.

"Yes, we have," said another, "here is father's old hat!"

And an old, worn-out hat popped up out of the hill for the shepherd boy. He at once put it on and saw an innumerable number of trolls hurrying toward the village, and went home himself, in order to get his dinner. But he could not understand how it happened that all the people whom he met passed close by him or nearly stepped on him; and when he spoke to any one they turned about in surprise, and did not answer him. At last he thought of the hat, and began to suspect that it might be due to the hat that people did not see him.

No more had this passed through his mind, than it occurred to him how pleasant it would be to see what was going on in the house where the feast was being given. So there he went, and was able to walk freely about among the guests, and see everything without being seen or noticed by anybody himself. And when the guests sat down to dinner, he could see an enormous number of trolls sitting among them, and helping themselves liberally to all the dishes, so that the people were entirely unable to

He put the hat on and saw a number of trolls hurrying toward the village.

understand what became of all the food that was brought on the table, and that seemed to disappear beneath their very hands. The shepherd boy hung about where there was something to get, and made a fine meal of everything among the eatables. And when he had not a bit of room left in which to stow away any more, it occurred to him that a good bite to eat would not harm his old mother at home. So he loaded himself with cake, roast, wine and other good things, and carried them home to her. Of course she was pleased when she saw all the good things; and, like her boy, she thought it would be pleasant to have more good things to eat the following day. So the boy saw to it that he carried home the best of all he could manage to lay hand on; and wherever he dipped in there was soon a hole in the dish, and whoever gave a feast was soon at the end of his resources. But that never worried our shepherd boy, who attended strictly to his own affairs.

At last, toward evening, the dance was about to begin. The boy, who had just gathered up another good armful of provisions, felt like looking on, and went up with the rest to the upper story. Here he had to squeeze into a corner, as well as he could, and look to it that no one stepped on him. Finally, he stood in front of the others, because he dared not trust himself in the closely-pressed crowd. There he stood and looked on, and was enjoying himself hugely; but just as the bride danced past him, her coat was spinning merrily around, and it knocked the hat from his head, and as soon as the hat was off, his invisibility had come to an end. There he stood, loaded down with all sorts of eatables; and when the people had recovered from their astonishment, he had to explain everything in detail. When he had done that, he had to take a good thrashing and resign himself to bringing back all the food he had stolen. So with the exception of the good dinner that he had already put away, he had no further profit for all his pains. As to the hat, it was never seen again.

Little May

ONCE UPON A TIME there was a little girl who herded sheep, and her name was May. Now the Prince of England decided, one day, that he would set forth and hunt up a wife for himself, and he passed by little May, as she was sitting by the edge of the road, herding her sheep. So he greeted her and said: "Good-day, little May, and how are you?"

"I am very well, for though I wear rags upon rags until I marry the king of England's son, then I shall wear gold upon gold."

"That will never happen, little May."

"Yes, indeed, it will happen."

So the prince traveled on to woo a bride, and he was not refused; but it was agreed that the bride should first visit him in order to see whom she was marrying. And when the foreign princess came, her way led her past little May, who was herding her sheep, and she greeted her and said: "How is the prince of England?"

"He is very well, but he has a stone set in the threshold of his door that tells everything one has ever done."

So the bride journeyed on. And when she came to the prince and trod on the stone, the stone said:

> "There's no truth in what she said
> For she already has been wed!"

When the prince heard that, he would hear no more of the princess, since he wished to marry a maid and not a widow, and the princess had to return whence she came.

Again the prince set forth to hunt up a bride, and once

more his way led him past little May. He greeted her and said:

"Good-day, little May. And how are you today?"

"I am very well, for though I wear rags upon rags until I marry the king of England's son, when I marry him I shall wear gold upon gold."

"That will never happen, little May."

"Yes, indeed, it will happen."

Then he journeyed on, and again his suit was successful. The foreign princess was willing to marry him, and it was agreed that she should go and visit him; for he always made this a condition.

Now on her way to the prince she passed little May. So she asked after the English prince, and May answered: "He is well, but he has a stone set in the threshold of his door that tells everything one has ever done."

When she entered the prince's home and trod on the stone, the stone said:

> "There's no truth in what she said
> Twice already she has wed!"

That would not answer, and of course the prince did not wish to have anything more to do with her. She was welcome to go back whence she came, for the prince had made up his mind to marry a maid and not a widow twice over.

So once more he set forth to hunt for a bride, and as usual, his way led him past little May. He greeted her and said: "How are you, little May?"

"I am very well, for though I wear rags over rags until I marry the king of England's son, when I marry him I shall wear gold over gold."

"That will never happen, little May."

"Yes, indeed, it will happen."

Thereupon the prince went his way, and came to the princess whom he wished to make his bride. His suit was successful, and it was agreed that she should come and visit him, and with this consolation he traveled back home again.

Now when the new bride came to visit him her way took her past little May, and she asked after the prince of England.

"Yes, he is well, but he has a stone set in the threshold of his door that tells everything one has ever done."

The princess went on, and when she trod on the stone, the stone said:

> "There's no truth in what she said
> Thrice already she has wed."

This was going from bad to worse, and the princess was at once sent home again.

So once more the prince had to start out on his wanderings; for he had made up his mind to take a wife. On the way he passed little May, who was herding her sheep.

"Good-day, little May, and how are you?"

"I am well, for though I wear rags over rags until I marry the king of England's son, then I shall wear gold over gold."

"That will never happen, little May."

"Yes, indeed, it will happen."

He traveled on and found a fourth princess; sued for her hand and was informed that he might have it. It was agreed that she was to pay him a visit, and then he traveled home again.

When the princess went to visit him, she inquired how the other three princesses had fared with the prince, and she had no mind to be the fourth one rejected. When she passed little May she first asked her how the king of England's son was.

"Oh, he is well, but he has a stone set in the threshold of his door that tells everything one has ever done."

So the princess asked whether she could not visit the prince in her place. They could change clothes, and she would mind the sheep for her in the meantime.

Little May was quite willing, and was dressed in the princess's clothes, and thus went to visit the prince. When she trod on the stone, the stone said:

> "This maid who visits you
> Is lovely, pure and true!"

"Well, at last the right one has come," thought the prince. "I have found the maid I have wished for so long." And in order that there might be no mistake, and that he would be sure to recognize her again, he wove a ring in her hair, and allowed her to travel home again for the present; for she was not to return until the wedding.

When little May had been dismissed by the prince, she changed clothes once more, and the princess went back to her people, and was glad that everything had gone so smoothly, for she was as much a widow as the rest.

When the time came for the prince to go to his bride, and celebrate the wedding, he passed little May as usual. He greeted her and said:

"How do you do, little May?"

"I am very well, for though I wear rags over rags until I marry the king of England's son, then I shall wear gold over gold." And as the king's son stood there and looked at her he noticed something gleaming in her hair. His curiosity aroused, he looked more closely to see what it might be, and found his own golden ring, which he had woven into it. Then he knew that she and no one else had visited him, and since he knew that she was a pure and good maiden, and he had already been deceived so many times, he determined to take her straight home with him and marry her. As for her sheep, any one who felt so in- clined might look after them. So they were married, and that is how it happened that little May secured the king of England's son after all, and could wear gold over gold.

The Princess on the Island

THERE ONCE REIGNED a king in England, who had an only son. It chanced that on a time a picture of the princess of Denmark came into the young prince's hands, and from that moment on he had no peace: she and none other was the woman he wished to marry.

So he went to his father and told him that he loved the princess of Denmark above everything, and wished to marry her. His father was entirely satisfied. "If England and Denmark stand together, there is no power on earth that can stand against them," he said. He at once wrote a letter to the Danish king and asked his daughter's hand for his son, who would succeed him as king of England. But the Danish king wrote back that his daughter was still a child, and that at all events, she should never be queen of England. This made the English king angry, and he wrote again, and said that the Danish princess must become his son's bride, though blood be spilt as a consequence. Thereupon the Danish king answered that it should never happen so long as there was a drop of blood left in a Dane.

So war broke out. The English prince came to Denmark with a great army and besieged the capital. But the Danish king sent his daughter away to an island. He gave her seven maidens and a little dog to keep her company, together with supplies for seven years. Then he had the castle on the island walled up, so that no one could get in or out.

When seven years had passed, the English prince had captured the city and slain the king. He established himself in the castle, visited all the rooms, and also came to

47

the princess's room. And there stood an ivory spinning-wheel whose spokes were of red gold. A fabric beautifully woven with birds, fishes and all sorts of beasts hung in the spindle; but it was unfinished. After the prince had the princess searched for and sought after for a long time, he bade proclaim throughout the country that she who could complete the fabric that hung from the spindle should be his queen. For he thought that the Danish princess would put in an appearance, once she knew she had nothing to fear from him.

Now there was a duke in the Danish land, whose daughter bore a close resemblance to the vanished princess, and who was a very skillful spinner. He told her to go to the castle and make the attempt; but the fabric had been woven with an art beyond her power to equal, and all that she wove turned out to be wrong.

In the meantime the princess, with her seven maids and the little dog, had been living in the walled-up castle on the island. They had eaten up their seven years' store of provisions, and began to suffer from hunger, so they tried to break through the wall; but it was slow work, and they were nearly dead of starvation, so little food was there left. Then, one after another, the seven maids who were with the princess leaped from the castle wall into the sea, that their mistress, whom they loved, might not perish of hunger. And with them went the little dog.

Meanwhile the princess killed mice in the castle, skinned them, hung up the skins and ate the flesh, and, just as the last of them was gone, she managed to break through the wall. Not far from the strand she saw a ship, waved to it and was taken on board. She was put ashore near her father's castle. Here she drew off her beautiful clothes, and wrapping herself in rags, went to the kitchen and asked whether they could use a scrub-woman. She made a good impression on the duke's daughter, and was engaged. So now the Danish princess stood in the kitchen of her father's castle and did the most menial work. On Saturday the scrub-woman took her pail of water into the weaving-room. As she stood there, admiring the artfully woven fabric in the spindle, the duke's daughter said to her that she had never in all her life woven so difficult a pattern. But the scrub-girl answered she felt confident she could complete the work.

"Well, if you can do that, I will give you a hundred dollars and make you chamber-maid," said the duke's daughter.

The princess pulled out all the strands which the other girl had woven incorrectly, and then began to spin rapidly. The prince could hear the spinning-wheel humming till it echoed through the whole castle, and in the course of a few days he was informed that the fabric was completed. Then he came and examined it. He could find no fault with it whatever, and now had to keep his word and marry the duke's daughter, though he had his serious doubts as to whether she really was the Danish princess.

The Danish princess had owned a horse named Blanca. It had been left to its own devices during the seven years the war had lasted, and had become so vicious that two men had to lead it to water with strong poles. The wedding was to take place on a Sunday, and the prince had given orders that his bride was to ride to the church on Blanca; for well he knew that none but the Danish princess would dare to ride Blanca. The duke's daughter did not dare to do so. She told the real princess, who had become a scrub-girl, to take off her wretched clothes, and put on her own bridal gown, and to ride to church with the prince in her stead. As a reward she would give her another hundred dollars.

The prince came and called for the princess, and took her with him. First they came to a bridge that creaked and groaned. Then the princess said:

> "Bridge, break not beneath the bride!
> You were the king, my father's pride!"

And the bridge became quiet.

"What did you say, heart of mine?" asked the prince.

"Nothing, my lord!" answered the princess.

Then they came to a gate, and before it lay a dog on a chain. The dog barked and growled. Then the princess said:

> "Dog, bark no more, but stand aside!
> You were the king, my father's pride!"

The dog stopped barking.

"What did you say, heart of mine?" asked the prince.

"Nothing, my lord!" answered the princess.

They went on and came to a dike. Here the princess said:

> "Below the dike the fish are gay,
> And merrily in the water play.
> Could red gold have bought the food they craved,
> My seven maids I mourn had been saved!"

"What did you say, little heart of my heart?" asked the prince. "Nothing, my lord!" replied the princess. And they rode on.

Far off in the distance the princess could see the island where she had dwelt for seven years. Then she said:

> "Gray mouse-skins hanging whence I fled,
> I drew you off with fear and dread.
> Had I not starved, I'd not have fed
> On mice, instead of goodly bread!"

"What did you say, little heart of my heart?" asked the prince.

"Nothing, my lord!" replied the princess.

At last they came to Blanca. Blanca kicked out, reared and was quite unmanageable. At last the princess said:

> "Blanca, Blanca, kneel for me,
> No other maid has ridden thee,
> Save her you see!"

No sooner had the horse heard the voice of the princess than it knelt for her, and she could mount it.

"What did you say, heart of my heart?" asked the prince.

"Nothing, my lord!" answered the princess. But the prince was happy, for now he knew that none other than the Danish princess was riding beside him. And when they reached the church the prince gave her his golden gloves, and made her vow that she, and she alone would give the gloves back to him should he ask for them.

Then they were betrothed, and rode back from the church to the castle. Here they were to change their clothes; and the princess stepped into the weaving-room while the duke's daughter stepped out in her stead. Now all thought there would be a great feast with many guests; but the prince declared that he did not feel just in the humor for a feast that day, and that the guests were to return on the morrow, when the wedding would be celebrated.

When evening came the prince and the duke's daughter went into the bridal chamber. Then the prince begged her to repeat to him what she had said on the bridge. The duke's daughter said that it was strange, she had forgotten everything that day; but she had a chamber-maid to whom she had confided all that she had said during the day, and she would be sure to know. She would ask her.

So the bride ran out to the princess, and said to her: "Listen, you little silly, what did you say on the bridge?" The princess repeated her words, and the duke's daughter returned to the prince and said:

> "Bridge, break not beneath the bride!
> You were the king, my father's pride!"

"Yes, that's what it was," said the prince, and she thought that the questioning was over. But the prince now asked her what was it she said to the dog. She told him that her heart was so taken up with love for him that she simply could not remember anything; but she would go at once to her chamber-maid and ask her. So she ran to the princess, and told her that her head would turn with all the speeches she was supposed to have made underway. "Now what was it that you said to the dog?" And the princess told her, and she went back to the prince and repeated:

> "Dog, bark no more, but stand aside!
> You were the king, my father's pride!"

"Yes, that's what it was," said the prince, "that is a wonderful chamber-maid you have."

The duke's daughter now thought that he would stop. But the prince also wanted to know what she had said at the dike. So she had to ask the princess again, and came back and told him:

> "Below the dike the fish are gay,
> And merrily in the water play.
> Could red gold have bought the food they craved,
> My seven maids I mourn had been saved!"

The prince said that her chamber-maid must have a good memory; but he still wanted to know what she had said when she looked at the island out in the sea. So once more she was obliged to go to the princess, very much annoyed at all the running to and fro she had to do. And she asked her: "What was it you said, you chatterbox, when you saw the island out at sea?" The princess did not like the way she addressed her; but kept her temper, and quietly repeated the words. And when the duke's daughter came back to the prince she had once more remembered what she had said:

> "Gray mouse-skins hanging whence I fled,
> I drew you off with fear and dread.
> Had I not starved, I'd not have fed
> On mice, instead of goodly bread!"

"Yes, that's what it was," said the prince; and now she thought that he would at last content himself. But the prince still wanted to know what she said to Blanca. Why, that had also completely slipped her memory; but the chamber-maid would be sure to recall it, since she had told it all to her when she came out of church.

Again she ran to the princess, and if she had not been angry before she was decidedly angry now: what did she mean by all the speeches she had been reciting to the prince while they were underway? One might imagine that she, the duke's daughter, had nothing else to do but run back and forth between them. "Tell me at once, what sort of speech did you make to him when you were to ride Blanca?" The princess still kept her temper, and told her the truth. And when the duke's daughter had the answer she went to the prince and repeated it to him:

> "Blanca, Blanca, kneel for me,
> No other maid has ridden thee,
> Save her you see!"

"Yes, that's what it was," said the prince. "Your chamber-maid has memory enough for two." So now the duke's daughter thought he would let her be. But no, the prince now insisted that she return to him the golden gloves that he had asked her to take charge of for him. She said that they were in her room, and that she would get them at once. When she came to the princess this time she was far more polite than before, and asked her for the gloves. But the princess said: no, she could not give them to her, since she had sworn an oath that she herself, and none other, would give back the gloves to the prince. The duke's daughter wrung her hands, and did not know what to do. Then the princess had an idea: they both would enter the bridal chamber, put out the lights, and give the prince his gloves; then she would slip from the room, and the duke's daughter would stay with the prince, and he would never notice the deception.

They went back together to the bridal chamber. The princess entered, put out the lights, and went up to the prince with the gloves. And then she wanted to slip from the room; but the prince held her arm, and said she would have to stay with him, and that whoever else might be in the room was to go out. In the morning the duke's daughter was sent back to her father; but in the castle they celebrated the wedding of the English prince with the Danish princess.

The Good Sword

ONCE UPON A TIME there was an old widower who had an only son, who lived with him. The old man was a poacher, and that is how he supported his son and himself. But when he had grown old, he became weaker and weaker, and sadly told his son that soon he would no longer be able to hunt for him, and that ere long he would have to die. His son comforted him, and assured him he would soon recover; but his father said no, ere long he would have to die, and he had nothing to leave him. What they had would just about do for his own funeral. Yet he had one possession that might prove to be a blessing to his son. It was only a sword, and badly rusted at that, but it would conquer any one against whom it was raised.

Before long the father died, and his son had to sell what he left in order to bury him. All that he kept of his inheritance was the rusty sword. Now he had to find work to do, and this was not easy, since he had never learned a trade, and at the best could only herd sheep. So he went to the village, and had to content himself with hiring out as a shepherd. His master sent him out with the sheep, and warned him to keep away from three meadows, which belonged to three mountain trolls. They lived on a hill known as "Troll's Mount," and if one of his sheep were to stray to their meadow, the mountain troll would come, and not only carry off the sheep, but their shepherd as well. As to his carrying off the shepherd, his master only said that to frighten the young fellow, because it was not true.

The new shepherd promised to take good care of the sheep, and so he did; for he lost not a single one, and his master was well content with him. Once he happened to think of his sword, and that it might be of use to help him should he have trouble with the mountain troll. And he determined to try it on him some time.

So one day he let his sheep stray into the first of the forbidden meadows, and at once the mountain troll, raging and roaring, rushed up to him, and asked who had allowed him to pasture his sheep in that meadow.

"I allowed myself to do it," said the young fellow, and when the mountain troll threatened to carry him off together with his sheep, he attacked him and struck him dead with his sword.

Now the first meadow belonged to him; but not long after the sheep felt like visiting the second meadow, and the young fellow let them go. Thereupon the second mountain troll rushed up to him in a towering rage, and the young fellow slew him, too. It was the same with regard to the third meadow, and the lad came home with his sheep, singing.

Now he had a fancy to see "Troll's Mount," and there he found three steeds, a red, a white and a yellow one, and three dogs, also red, white and yellow in color. And for each steed there was a saddle, and a full suit of armor as well, and they, too, were red, white and yellow in color. Besides, there was fodder for the horses, and food for the dogs, and gold and silver in abundance. The shepherd lad was naturally much pleased with all the splendor that had come into his possession, and went home singing. Then his master had him told by the farm-hand that although he was extraordinarily well satisfied with him, he wished he would stop singing. The young fellow could not see what harm his singing did. And at first the farm-hand did not want to tell him the true reason, and said he ought to be willing to stop because his master wished it. But at last the young fellow induced the farm-hand to tell him why he was not to sing, though he forbade him to tell any one else.

It seems that great sorrow reigned throughout the land,

because the king had been compelled to betroth his three daughters to three trolls. Soon the trolls were to come to fetch them, and the king had promised a third of the kingdom to any man who could deliver one of them, and the hand of the princess he delivered as well. "It is for that reason you must not sing here in town, although out in the fields it makes no difference," said the farm-hand.

The young fellow could not help thinking about the story of the poor princesses, and it occurred to him that perhaps he might be able to save them. He could leave his sheep to their own devices with a clear conscience, since now he had nothing to fear from the mountain trolls, and he went to town to find out what was being said about the calamity that was due. There he learned on which day the oldest princess would be led out to the troll, and putting on his red armor, he mounted his red steed, and with the red dog rode out to the place where the troll was to receive the princess. She came driving up in a coach, and the coachman climbed a tree in his fear of the troll. And at the very moment the red knight came riding up, a three-headed troll rose out of the sea. The knight rode up to him, hewed off all three of his heads with his rusty sword, cut out their tongues, and rode off again.

Then the coachman climbed down from his tree, and threatened to kill the princess unless she promised to say that he had delivered her. She had to promise, he gathered up the heads, and they drove home.

Eight days later the second princess was driven out, and all happened as before. The coachman sought safety in a tree, and a yellow knight came riding up on a yellow horse followed by a yellow dog. Then out of the sea rose a monster with six heads. The knight cut off the heads, tore out the tongues, and rode off again. This coachman also threatened this princess, and demanded she say he had delivered her.

Eight days later the youngest princess was driven out to be handed over to her troll, and again all happened as before. The coachman climbed a tree, and a white knight

At the very moment the red knight came riding up,
a three-headed troll rose out of the sea.

appeared on a white horse, followed by a white dog. The troll rose out of the sea and he had nine heads; but the knight hewed them all off, and tore out their tongues. When the princess saw that he had delivered her she took off her chain of gold and tried to throw it around his neck; but it fell on his head. He had curly hair, and feeling something on his head, he gathered it up and wound it in his hair, and put his helmet over it so that no one could see it. Then he rode away. This coachman acted just as the others had, and compelled the princess to say that he had delivered her.

The greatest joy now reigned in the castle, and all three princesses were to be married on the same day. The young fellow by now had had his fill of sheep-herding, and took leave of his master, who did not like to let him go, since he had never done so well with his sheep as when the young fellow had had them in charge. But there was nothing he could do; his shepherd wanted to go, and so they settled their accounts and off he went.

He went to another village near-by, and took a room in the inn, where he heard much talk of the splendor with which the coming triple wedding was to be celebrated. The host of the tavern mentioned how pleasant it would be to have a chance to taste a bit of the fine wheat bread that was baked in the castle.

"Well," said the young fellow, "that's not at all impossible. My dog can get it," and he sent his red dog to get some wheat bread. The dog ran to the castle and scratched at one door after another. The people opened their doors for him, and in this way he reached the room where the wheat bread lay. He seized a loaf of bread, and the king said that they were to let him keep it, so he came safely home with it. Then the tavern-keeper talked about how pleasant it would be to sample the roast that came from the kitchens of the castle. The young fellow sent his yellow dog to fetch some of the roast, and the dog ran to the castle, sniffed about for the kitchen, seized the whole roast and ran off with it, and the king gave order to let him go. Now when the tavern-keeper saw the roast, he wished to have wine as well, and the young fellow sent his white dog to fetch it. And he actually found the wine-cellar, took a bottle of wine, and ran into the room where all the princesses and their husbands-to-be were seated.

When the youngest princess saw the white dog she clapped her hands, and said that his master had delivered her. Her betrothed grew angry, and said that hitherto she had always declared that he had delivered her, and what did she mean by saying what she did? But she insisted that the white dog's master had delivered her. So the king sent out men to follow the dog, in order to discover his master and bring him to the castle. The dog ran as fast as ever he could, so that the men could scarcely follow him. Yet they reached the tavern, puffing and groaning, and told the young fellow that he was to come to the castle. When he got there he asked whether his dog had misbehaved in the castle in any way that called for punishment. He himself knew of nothing he could have done.

"Yes," said the king, "he has stolen a bottle of wine. Not that that matters; but you must come into the great hall."

The young fellow excused himself, and said that he was not used to meeting such fine people. But he could not help himself, for the king insisted that he enter. So he went into the great hall, and no sooner had the youngest princess seen him than she declared that he was her deliverer. When her betrothed grew angry, and the others would not believe it, she asked him whether he did not have her chain of gold. So he drew it from his curls, and all saw that it was the princess's own. But her betrothed spoke of the nine heads which he had. Whereupon the young fellow produced the nine tongues for the nine heads, and all recognized that he had delivered the three princesses. The three deceivers were beheaded, and the true deliverer received the youngest princess and the third part of the kingdom at once, and after her father's death the remainder of it.